An imprint of Starfish Bay Publishing
www.starfishbaypublishing.com

THE TALE OF MR. MOON

© Emily May, 2021
ISBN 978-1-76036-133-4
First Published 2021
Printed in China

Sincere thanks to Elyse Williams from Starfish Bay Children's Books for her creative efforts in preparing this edition for publication.

The TALE of MR. MOON

By Emily May

When the sun turns off her light,
Mr. Moon stands tall and bright.
He lights the night with his powerful beams,
to keep the nightmares from our dreams.

Although he loves his wonderful view,
Mr. Moon's been feeling blue.
He is up so late when we're all asleep,
so he has no one, not even a sheep.

In an old house far out of sight,
a little girl wakes late in the night.

Her name is Katy, and though she's quite small,
her ideas are the grandest of all.

Spotting the moon sad in the sky,
Katy sets off to find out why.

"Mr. Moon," she calls, "please shine bright.
Why are you upset tonight?"

But up in the sky so far away,

he can't quite hear what she's trying to say.

Closer and closer, he leans into the air,

then all of a sudden, he falls off his chair!

He falls past the stars, the birds, and the bees.

He tumbles past mountains and plummets through trees.

Down down down, till he can
fall no more,

and then with a THUMP,
he lands on the floor.

The town is woken up with a jump.
What could have caused that thump?
In shock, the townsfolk stop and stare
at the moon now lying there.

The moon is in pieces. There's no time to waste!

Off they rush to get tape and some paste.

Using a ladder and the big pot of glue,

they fix Mr. Moon until he's good as new.

The townsfolk are happy. They all cheer, "HOORAY!"
Now to get home before night becomes day.

Mr. Moon isn't sure what to do,

when a little voice cries, "I can help you."

The townsfolk hurry back to their homes
and return with the longest ladders they own.
Working together, they all start to sing
as they tie the ladders together with string.

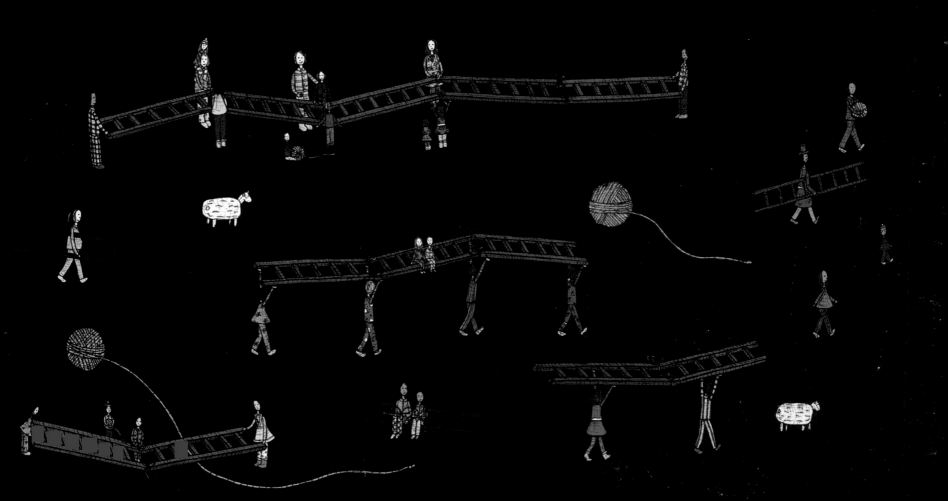

They work so hard that, in no time at all,
the ladder is over 500 feet tall!
Stacked up in a line, so big and so neat,
they PUSH up those ladders to Mr. Moon's seat.

When it's time to leave, Mr. Moon starts to cry,
"I will miss my new friends when I'm back in the sky."

Then Katy climbs up and says in his ear,
"You can still use the ladders to visit us here."

With a smile on his face, Mr. Moon says goodbye
and climbs back up to his home in the sky.
Happy, he sits and shines as before.
He WILL see his friends down on earth once more.

That's why in the sky, about twelve times a year,
it seems Mr. Moon has disappeared.
But really, he's gone to visit his friends,
which is where he may be when this story ends.